# Ready, Aim, Fire!

# Titles in
## the Storykeepers series

# Ready, Aim, Fire!

Brian Brown and Andrew Melrose

ZondervanPublishingHouse
*Grand Rapids, Michigan*

*A Division of HarperCollinsPublishers*

For Diane

# Contents

# Chapter 1

# Mordecai in Trouble

Mordecai limped as he strolled slowly down a cobbled alleyway of Rome's Merchant District.

"Here! Old man! Over here! A special balm for that leg of yours!" cried a man at a stall fragrant with the smell of herbs and spices.

Mordecai stopped. He looked up and down the alleyway.

"Come, come. I have just what you need for that leg of yours," the shopkeeper said, walking toward Mordecai, grabbing his arm, and pulling him toward the small open stall. "It's an old remedy all the way from Capernaum."

"From Capernaum, eh? Well, who can resist," said Mordecai, bending over to breathe in the aromas from the spices in the herbalist's stall. "I have an important message I must deliver, but I guess it can wait a little."

Mordecai sat on a stool in front of the herbalist's stall and pulled up his toga, exposing two skinny, knobby legs.

"Ooh, that is a bad scar. What is it from?" the herbalist asked as he dipped two fingers into a jar, then began rubbing the ointment onto Mordecai's leg.

"An old war wound," Mordecai said, looking down at the darkened scar on the calf of his leg. He glanced quickly at the alley, as if he was afraid of something. "That soldier sure had it in for me that day, but he shot low. His arrow went right through my leg and stuck there. Had to break it off to get it out. That's why I walk every day now. I walk out the stiffness. Mmmm. That does feel better. It feels warm."

"Yes, yes. I sell a lot of this," the shopkeeper said, continuing to rub the ointment onto Mordecai's leg.

"But I must be going. How much do I owe you?" Mordecai said, carefully looking up and down the alleyway. When he looked back, he saw that the shopkeeper had drawn the outline of a secret sign in the ointment on his leg. Mordecai looked at him anxiously, fearing a trap.

"Don't be afraid," the man whispered. "I know that you are Mordecai, the Messenger. I have been watching for you."

With his hand he erased the outline of the fish that he had drawn on Mordecai's leg. The sign of the fish was secret. The sign meant that he was a Christian. Or a spy.

A Roman soldier was standing next to a vegetable stall across the way, but he did not seem to be paying any attention to them. Still, a Christian had to be careful.

Christians were not liked in Rome. In fact, the Emperor Nero hated them and had set fires all over Rome trying to burn them out of their homes.

The herbalist leaned closer to Mordecai and, pointing at the scar, said, "Where did this happen?"

"In Galilee, near the ruins of the old town of Sepphoris, near Nazareth," Mordecai said.

"Yes, yes, I've heard of it," the shopkeeper said. "I've heard stories. Tell me what really happened."

Mordecai looked around again, then carefully studied the herbalist. One couldn't be too careful.

Then he began the tale. "Taxes were terrible. The Roman soldiers were taking our grain. Our people worked so hard and had nothing left. It was all going to the Romans. Some, the freedom fighters, were saying that we are governed by God, not by the Romans. That started the rebellion.

"At first there was just a lot of guerilla fighting. Small skirmishes, that's all. Just enough to annoy the soldiers, but nothing big.

"Then came that awful day," Mordecai said, looking down at his sandals. He rocked a little on the stool, remembering that day in Galilee. It was the last time he saw his father. He remembered how the Roman soldiers had come, carrying lighted torches. He heard again the screams from that day so long ago.

In a low voice he said, "I'll never forget what the Romans did that day at Sepphoris." Suddenly fearful, he stood up. "I must leave."

"Oh, please. Stay a while longer. Tell me more," the shopkeeper said. "You are safe here. I'll keep watch." He dipped into the ointment again and motioned for Mordecai to sit down.

"It happened about the time Jesus and his parents returned from Egypt," Mordecai said, looking down the alley, then up the other way. "Some of the men of Sepphoris got fed up with being pushed around by the Romans.

"They were fighting men. So one day they raided the Roman army's weapons storehouse. They stole swords, shields, and spears. After that, they won a few small battles against the Romans. They were so sure they were right, so sure they'd win and we'd all eventually be free."

"And?" the shopkeeper said when Mordecai paused.

"King Herod Antipas heard about the trouble and knew he had to act. The rebels were winning. If he didn't stop the uprising in Galilee, the Roman Emperor would surely punish him.

"So one day Herod's men arrived in Sepphoris with burning torches and marched from house to house, one by one, setting them all on fire. Men, women, and children started screaming and running, trying to flee the flames. But the soldiers caught them. They showed no mercy.

"They rounded up the people and chained them. They led them away from their burned-out homes … into slavery." Mordecai looked carefully at the shopkeeper. "Nero is doing the same now to the Christians here in Rome," said the shopkeeper with a sigh.

"It is awful now. It must have been terrible then," the shopkeeper said.

"Oh, yes, it was," murmured Mordecai cautiously. "Some escaped to the hills and told the freedom fighters what had happened. Everyone who escaped knew they could never go back home."

Mordecai paused again. "My father was one of the lucky ones. He escaped into the hills. But we never saw him again.

"That day the soldiers split up whole families. Husbands and wives were separated. Mothers and fathers lost their children, and some of these children were even separated from their brothers and sisters.

"My brother and I escaped. Over the years, we kept looking, but never found our father. I don't know what happened to him.

"The freedom fighters stayed together for a long time after Sepphoris. My brother and I soon joined the fighting. That's when I got hit by the arrow. The Romans continued to hunt us down."

"But you are here, in Rome, now," the shopkeeper said. "Why? Are you not afraid of the Roman soldiers? What they will do if they find you?"

Mordecai smiled. "One day we saw Jesus in Galilee. We were with others who had gathered to hear him. He said we should love our enemies, even the Romans. At first I thought, that's easy for you to say, but the more he spoke, the more he made sense.

"Something else happened that day, too. Do you know, he took a couple of fish—just two small fish—and five small barley loaves and fed all the people who had gathered on that mountainside. There must have been five thousand there. And we had food left over! Twelve baskets of food!"

"Yes, I heard about it," said the herbalist. "Ben the baker told us about it a while back."

"Ah, so you know Ben and the Storykeepers. That's who I'm going to see. I'm a courier for the underground that Ben and Helena help to run. I do some of the more dangerous work."

"Once a rebel, always a rebel, eh?"

"Well, you can't give up all your old ways," Mordecai said with a grin. "And I like to think that I'm putting mine to good use."

Suddenly Nihilus, Nero's top soldier, stepped out from the shade of an old, gnarled olive tree nearby. "How very touching," he sneered. "Christian, you're under arrest!"

# Chapter 2

# Halt!

Mordecai jumped up, knocking over the stool. Before Nihilus could say more, Mordecai was off and running, dodging around traders' stalls and pushing through the crowded marketplace, his toga flapping around his skinny legs.

"Halt in the name of Caesar!" Nihilus shouted. But Mordecai pressed forward, bumping against passersby and sending a flock of chickens scattering. At his age, he couldn't move quickly for long, so he moved cleverly, keeping as many obstacles as he could between himself and the Roman soldiers who had joined the chase.

Ahead, he spotted the massive arches of one of the great Roman aqueducts. *There*, he thought. And he began to run. Rome had fourteen aqueducts with long stone canals on top that carried water from the nearby hills to wells and pools all over the city.

Darting around a corner, Mordecai slipped and fell, face first, into a muddy puddle. "Argggh!" he groaned, picking himself up. He was covered with mud from head to toe, and the hot midday sun quickly began baking it dry and hard.

Frantic, he looked for a place to hide. Then he noticed a ring of life-sized statues of Caesar nearby. He grinned. Perhaps his mud was a blessing and would make good camouflage. "'Statues' was a game I played as a child, in Galilee. Little did I know it would come in handy now that I'm a man."

Quickly, he tucked himself in beside a statue of an emperor and didn't move a muscle. He looked very serious.

The soldiers peered around the viaduct arch, searching in vain.

"He must be here somewhere," said Nihilus impatiently. "I want that Christian. Find him."

A very fat soldier called Stouticus bit off a piece of honey biscuit. "We'd better find him," he grumbled to the other soldiers. "Nihilus won't think twice about punishing us if we don't. He is one evil centurion. He has a wicked temper. I should know."

"And don't come back without him!" Nihilus shouted. "I whip the soldiers who do not carry out my orders!"

"See what I mean?" Stouticus said under his breath, knowing only too well that Nihilus was a man of his word. "Keep searching."

Mordecai stood perfectly still as Stouticus and the other soldiers continued their search.

Stouticus looked right at Mordecai. And Mordecai's

brown eyes looked right back at him.

"What's this?" he cried, raising his sword.

Quicker than Stouticus could blink an eye, Mordecai reached up and pulled the soldier's helmet down over his face. Then he ran.

"There he is!" shouted Nihilus. "You dolts! He's getting away! After him, or I will flay you all!"

"Here we go again," said Mordecai, as the chase resumed. "Luckily my leg feels better."

Mordecai skipped over obstacles and shimmied around corners.

"Just like the old days," he said with a chuckle. "Those soldiers may think they have me, but you don't catch an old Zealot without a struggle."

# Chapter 3

# Up in the Trees

"I love climbing trees," said nine-year-old Anna. "But I never thought I would *be* one."

Cyrus, a young African juggler, laughed and reached over to plop a clump of leaves on Anna's head. "You missed a spot."

"Why thank you, Cyrus," said Anna.

The two were barely visible in the branches of an old olive tree. The tree was in the garden of a large home in the Market District. The home belonged to a Christian called Darius. Anna and Cyrus adjusted their leaf and twig disguises. This was more than a game. They were lookouts.

Darius's house was the temporary home of the Christian underground. The Christians were to meet there that night. Ben the baker was going to tell a story.

Anna and Cyrus were watching for Mordecai. They giggled as they shifted in the branches of the tree, tugging and poking at each other's disguises.

A few feet below them was sixteen-year-old Zak, standing on top of the garden wall. Zak was Ben's apprentice at the bakery and liked to take charge. He looked up, irritated, when some olives dropped on his head. "Hey, you two, stop fooling around. We have a job to do. Any sign of the courier yet?"

"Not yet, Zak," Anna replied.

"Well, keep a sharp eye out. And fix your camouflage, I can still see you. And stop smiling! Olive trees do *not* have teeth."

Anna and Cyrus muffled their laughter with handfuls of leaves. "I am very fond of Zak," whispered Anna, "but he is so serious. Especially today, for some reason."

"Yes, I've noticed," said Cyrus.

Anna and Cyrus snickered again. Zak glared up at them. Acting innocent, they made their faces straight and kept still.

Zak then spotted Justin, who was thirteen, crossing the courtyard in front of Darius's house, adjusting his fruit merchant disguise. "Justin," he called out, "why aren't you in position?"

"I'm going, I'm going. Don't get your toga in a twist."

Zak wrung his hands in exasperation. "How am I supposed to work with such a bunch of amateurs?" he muttered, shifting nervously from foot to foot. "Don't they know who we're expecting today?"

Against a wall of the courtyard, Ben, Helena, and four-year-old Marcus were in position alongside another fruit stand, an empty stand. They were leaning against the wall.

"Ben," said Marcus, as he looked up at the jolly baker.

"Yes, Marcus."

"What's wrong with Zak? He's always bossy, but today he's crabby too."

"Well, Marcus," Ben answered, "the courier we are expecting is Zak's Uncle Mordecai."

"Really?" Marcus asked.

"Yes," Helena answered. "And Zak wants to make a good impression. He knows his uncle was a great leader among the Zealots."

"Here he comes!" Anna called, nearly falling out of the olive tree. "But he's being chased by soldiers!"

Zak became flustered. He stepped left, then right, then left again. Then he snapped to attention and shouted, "Positions, everybody, positions! Get to your positions!"

Mordecai puffed and panted as he ran toward them. "Phew! I'm getting too old for this running. Ben said my daily stroll would be a perfect disguise for a courier. Nobody said anything about a daily run."

The soldiers puffed and panted after him. Their swords rattled and their feet pounded on the cobblestones. Stouticus in particular found it hard going. He couldn't keep up with the rest of them. "Oh, dear!" he wheezed. "Dear, oh, dear. All this running...and on an empty stomach too. Breakfast must have been hours ago. Soldiers should have tea breaks or at least time for a snack. The smell of all this fruit and bread is making me hungry."

"After him!" shouted Nihilus, who had caught up to Stouticus and was passing him. "He must not get away! After him, or I will flay you all, then feed you to the lions … and a pretty feast you will be too, Stouticus!"

"Oh, dear, dear me!" muttered Stouticus as he picked up the speed.

Anna and Cyrus watched the chase coming toward them from the safety of the olive tree. "I don't think he's going to make it," Cyrus said anxiously. "He's limping!"

"Okay! Pay attention, everyone!" called Zak. "You know the contingency plan. I'll activate the emergency barricade!"

Zak got his bow and arrow ready, then waited for his Uncle Mordecai to run through the archway leading to this section of the marketplace. As Mordecai came through the entrance, running toward a cart laden with precariously balanced pots and barrels marked "olive oil," Zak took aim. One of the pots had a crude target etched on the side, and Zak had it square in his sights. Only he could save his Uncle Mordecai now.

But Zak was nervous. Very nervous. What if he missed? His brow was moist with sweat. Even his hands were sweaty and began to shake.

Zak tried to steady the bow. But there was his uncle. Right in front of him! In the way! And before he knew what he had done, Zak fired … too soon. The arrow whizzed past the target, missing his uncle by a whisker.

Zak was shaking with fear and dismay. As he fumbled for another arrow, Ben snatched up his own bow and, with pinpoint accuracy, fired an arrow through a slit in the courtyard wall.

"Bull's-eye!" cheered Anna and Cyrus from the olive tree.

The pot shattered and spilled its oil over the edge of the cart. This, in turn, upset the fine balance of the precarious load, causing the cart to tip. The barrels of olive oil tumbled out of the cart, blocking the entrance to the marketplace just as Nihilus and his men tried to follow Mordecai through the archway.

Anna and Cyrus were giggling out of control. It was the funniest sight they had ever seen. Nihilus and his men were slipping and sliding on the oil, slamming against each other, swinging their arms to keep their balance, and grabbing hold of anything to stay up.

"Whoa!" shouted Stouticus, the last to arrive, as he, too, started slipping on the oil. The other soldiers could only stare as the enormous bulk, feet spread, slid toward them, knocking them down like bowling pins. They ended up in the weirdest positions. When Stouticus finally landed, there was an almighty thump as he settled firmly and squarely on Nihilus.

"Get off me, you mule-brained, overweight muttonhead!" screamed Nihilus. "Get off me and get after that Christian!"

"Psst! Mordecai," whispered Justin, as loud as he dared. "This way, quickly. Before the soldiers get back into action!"

"Ah, young Justin. At last. I didn't recognize you there at the fruit stand," said Mordecai.

"Quick, get behind my stall," Justin said.

"Anything you say, youngster," said Mordecai gratefully, looking over his shoulder as the soldiers, now shiny with oil, were getting up.

Seeing that Mordecai was safe, Anna whispered a loud "Now!" and Ben activated the second part of the plan. He and Helena shoved on the side of their stand, and Justin and his stand, with Mordecai hiding behind it, swung around a full 180 degrees, wall and all. In their place appeared an empty stand.

"Wow! Neat trick," said Mordecai, as he looked around inside the courtyard.

Justin smiled. "It was Zak's idea."

When Nihilus and the soldiers finally got to the empty replacement stand, Mordecai had vanished. Nihilus was livid.

"I'll get you Christians!" he shouted, not knowing if anyone was listening. "I'll get you, you'll see! You Christians can't escape Roman justice forever!"

## Chapter 4

# Safe Houses, Safe Kids

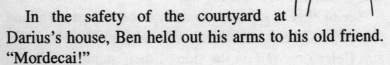

In the safety of the courtyard at Darius's house, Ben held out his arms to his old friend. "Mordecai!"

"Ben, my friend," Mordecai said, hugging him warmly. "And Helena, how good it is to see you."

"Mordecai," said Helena, "we're so glad to have you with us."

"Not as glad as I am to be here, Helena. For a moment there, I didn't think I'd make it! Now where's that nephew of mine?"

Around the corner, Zak was firing arrow after arrow right into the bull's-eye of a practice target.

"Zak, what are you doing?" asked Ben, a little perplexed. "Don't you want to see your Uncle Mordecai? He's waiting for you."

Zak, without stopping, said, "I can't believe I missed that shot. He must be so disappointed in me."

"But Zak, everyone misses a shot now and then."

"You don't understand, Ben. My father was one of the

greatest leaders the Zealots ever had. He was a marksman. He wouldn't have missed that shot."

Just then Mordecai came around the corner. "Zak! There you are."

"Uncle Mordecai. Watch this." Zak raised his bow, took careful aim, but again the butterflies danced in the pit of his stomach, and his hands began to shake. This time he missed the target altogether.

"I don't understand … this never happens," Zak wailed in dismay.

"Well, you hit the mark when it counted. You saved my neck back there."

Little Marcus looked up, wide-eyed, and said, "I thought it was Ben who hit the … oomph!"

"Hush, Marcus," hissed his older brother, Justin, clamping his hand over little Marcus's mouth.

Mordecai hugged his nephew, then held Zak at arm's length, smiling at this boy who was now almost as tall as his father had been. "You know, Zak, you are the image of your father, God rest his soul. And I'll bet you're every bit the leader he was too."

Zak smiled, his nervousness disappearing with his uncle's compliments. "Well, I try," he said bashfully.

"Which reminds me, I have something for you." Mordecai reached into a pouch that hung from the belt of his toga and pulled out a bronze Star of David. "Your father wanted you to have this when you were old enough. I think that time has come." Mordecai hung the medallion around Zak's neck.

"Thank you, Uncle Mordecai," said Zak, holding back tears of pride. "I promise I will be worthy of it."

"I know you will be," said his uncle, hugging him again, then ruffling his hair with his hand. "Always remember, your father was a very special man."

Cyrus, who was watching, fiddled with the beanbags he used for juggling. It was times like this when he missed his own parents. Anna, Justin, and Marcus also fidgeted uncomfortably. They had all lost their parents. They had been living on the streets of Rome when Ben and Helena took them in and gave them a home.

"Mordecai," said Cyrus at last, "did you really live through the Zealot uprising in Galilee?"

"And did you really defeat a Roman garrison?" added Anna.

"Tell us about the freedom fighters in Judea," chipped in Justin.

Mordecai smiled at the children, but Zak quickly butted in: "Enough! Uncle Mordecai doesn't have time to sit around and entertain a bunch of children."

"Why, of course I do," countered Mordecai. "Zak, you must remember what Jesus said about the way we should treat children."

"What'd he say, what'd he say?" Marcus begged. Being the youngest and often teased by the others, he liked to hear the stories about children.

"Well, Marcus," said Mordecai, taking the eager

youngster onto his knee, "one day Jesus and his disciples were on the road to Jerusalem. It had been a long, sweltering journey. Even though the sun was beginning to set, it was still hot and dusty. The disciples had become irritable and were quarreling with one another.

"Just as the sun was setting, Jesus arrived at a small house by the side of the road. A man was standing outside with his wife and children, two boys and a young girl. They welcomed Jesus and his disciples and invited them to stay for supper. Soon, everyone was sitting around the table, eating. The children, when they finished eating, went to play on the floor, in front of the fireplace. The adults lingered at the table. After a while, Jesus looked at his disciples and asked: 'What were you arguing about earlier?'

"The disciples exchanged looks and were embarrassed. They were too ashamed to answer. As it turned out, they had been arguing about which of them was the most important.

"Jesus said nothing at first, then beckoned to his host's youngest son. He picked up the boy and tossed him playfully into the air. His brother and sister looked on, laughing excitedly. Jesus then sat the boy on his knee and spoke to his disciples.

"'I have already told you that my kingdom belongs to people who are like this child.'

"The disciples, still feeling ashamed, all nodded their understanding.

"You see," Mordecai continued, "the disciples knew how important children were to Jesus because of something that had happened before."

"What was that?" asked Marcus.

"Well, outside someone else's house, Jesus had been talking with a group of adults when some parents and their children tried to get to see Jesus. The children were excited, smiling and giggling, and the disciples formed a blockade to keep the noisy group back, away from Jesus.

"When Jesus saw this, he said, 'Let the boys and girls come to me. Don't stop them. Anyone who does not accept God's kingdom like a little boy or girl will not get inside.'

"So the disciples stepped aside and let the children rush forward. The disciples soon noticed how happy Jesus was, sitting among the children, talking to them, smiling and ruffling their hair, just like I'm ruffling yours, Marcus. So you see, Zak, Jesus holds children in very high regard."

"So do I, Uncle. What good is a leader without his followers?" Zak polished his new medallion, then turned to the others, shouting, "All right everybody! Atten-SHUN!"

Justin, Anna, Cyrus, and Marcus all snapped to attention.

"It's time to show Uncle Mordecai how efficiently we can set up for tonight's meeting," Zak said. "Let's MOVE OUT!"

Ben, Helena, and Mordecai exchanged amused glances as Zak marched his young troops out the door and into the courtyard.

Outside, Zak began barking commands. "Justin, break out the torches. Anna, Cyrus, get the benches from the storage room. Marcus, assemble more camouflage for the lookouts. MOVE IT!"

"You know, Mordecai," said Ben, shaking his head, "I think Zak may have missed the point of your story."

"Hurry up with those benches!" they heard Zak yell.

"Yes, Ben," said Mordecai, "I think you're right."

# Chapter 5

# Nero's Palace

Nero was strolling about in a vast room in his Imperial Palace, rubbing his hands with glee. "Marvelous, simply marvelous. This model of Rome is so real I can almost smell the market. And oh, how I hate that smell. For some reason it always reminds me of Christians. And if there is one thing I hate worse than the smell of the market, it's Christians. All that piety and idolization of a mere carpenter's son makes my stomach churn.

"Snivilus! Where should I build my lovely new Pantheon? Try over there, Snivilus. No, not there, over there! Can't you see where I am pointing?"

"Yes, Caesar, phew! Over there, Caesar. Right you are. A wonderful spot, if I may say so. You won't be able to smell the market from there," Snivilus said, groveling as he struggled to carry a very heavy marble miniature of Nero's new Pantheon to the new location. Nero had commissioned the city architects to design a new temple to all the gods.

Just then, Nihilus entered the room. "Hail, Caesar!"

"Ah, Centurion Nihilus. I understand you lost another Christian courier in the Merchant District today," Nero said.

Nihilus nodded. "Caesar," he said, "the district is riddled with secret passages and tunnels. It's impossible to patrol. Would that you'd allow me to burn it to the ground."

"Hmmm! Burn it to the ground, eh," said Nero, stroking his chin thoughtfully. He surveyed his model again.

"The Merchant District would provide a perfect spot for my new Pantheon," said Nero, as he cleared a space, shoving the miniatures to one side. "Don't just stand there, Snivilus!"

"No, Caesar. I'm coming, Caesar," panted Snivilus. Once again, he picked up the heavy marble miniature of Nero's new Pantheon and carried it back to the other side of the room.

"But, Caesar," interrupted another of Nero's centurions, Tacticus. "A fire in the Merchant District could kill hundreds of people!"

"Yes," gloated Nero darkly. "Wouldn't that be wonderful! Nihilus, do you have a plan?"

"As a matter of fact, I do." Nihilus clapped twice and a soldier appeared with a model of a nasty looking catapult with a golden, hand-shaped scoop. "I call it the 'Wrath of Caesar.' It is perfect for those hard-to-start infernos."

"Fascinating," said Nero eagerly, his beady eyes

widening in anticipation. "Let me try it."

Nero snatched the catapult from the officer and set it on the model of Rome. Then he loaded a scrunched-up wad of parchment into the scoop. Nihilus lit the parchment, and Nero took aim. "FIRE!" he shouted, giggling at his own pun.

Snivilus, who had been leaning against the model of the Pantheon, mopping his brow and trying to catch his breath, suddenly looked up to see Nero's fireball heading straight toward him.

"Yeow!" he yelled, diving for the floor. The fireball narrowly missed him and landed on the model, right in the middle of the Merchant District.

"Oh, I like it! I like it! Reload me!" Nero cackled with glee.

As Nero and Nihilus continued to play with the catapult, another soldier watched the demonstration with some concern. It was Tacticus, a soldier that Anna had rescued in the catacombs.

Tacticus moved to the corner of the room where Nero's servant Darius was dusting. Leaning over, he whispered into the servant's ear, "You must get word to Ben. He'll be at your house tonight."

Darius looked stunned. "H-how ... what ... don't know what you mean!"

"I haven't time to explain. Nero may hear us. We mustn't let the fish get fried."

"Fried fish!" Darius glanced over at Nero, who

already had four or five small fires burning on the model of Rome. His eyes widened at the sight.

"I'll do what I can to stall Nihilus. Go as soon as you can," Tacticus urged.

Darius nodded fearfully, his eyes fixed on the flames dancing on the model of Rome.

Nero continued to laugh as the miniature of Rome burned. "Soon, Christians, soon you too will be burning," he cried.

The fire crackled and sparked, and the flames cast an evil glow over Nero's twisted features.

"Burn, Christians, burn!" Nero cried.

# Chapter 6

# **The Blind Man**

"Well done, men," boomed a very smug-looking Nihilus. "Caesar likes your work." He was standing outside the Imperial Palace, inspecting the awesome catapult that would soon destroy the Merchant District ... and the Christians hiding there.

"Gracious!" said Stouticus. "Praise ... and from Nihilus. He *must* be pleased. Perhaps he will reward us with a feast. Dinner seems such a long time ago. All this catapult building has left me a bit peckish."

"Now let's get it over to the hill overlooking the Merchant District," Nihilus ordered.

"Oh, dear, more work," Stouticus sighed. "I knew there had to be a catch."

The soldiers harnessed a team of six horses to the giant catapult, but even then the troop had to help push it up the hill.

"Why didn't we just get more horses?" groaned Stouticus.

Cyrus and Anna are hiding in a tree

Zak misses but Ben hits the barrels

**Nihilus slips on the oil**

**Zak's uncle Mordecai has stories to tell**

"Zak, this belonged to your father!"

Blind Bartimaeus called: "Son of David, help me!"

**"I have a secret weapon," Nihilus told Caesar**

**Suddenly a huge ball of fire dropped from the sky**

**Putting out the fire**

**Sometimes helping people gets you into trouble**

**Jesus healed a crippled man**

**The man was happy**

**The gang jump to the wagon**

**Zak doesn't miss this time**

**The bust crashes into the aqueduct**

**The city was saved from the fire**

"Stouticus," snarled Nihilus. "Get some weight behind it. It's not as if you don't have some to spare."

Stouticus wheezed and mopped his brow with a rag. While his eyes were covered, Darius sneaked past the convoy and ran on ahead to warn Ben and the others.

\* \* \*

At Darius's house, Anna and Cyrus were again in the lookout tree, this time with little Marcus.

"Hey, Anna!" shouted Cyrus. "Are my leaves on straight?" Cyrus giggled as he preened himself.

"Yeah, but you need more twigs. Here, let me help." Anna and Marcus both giggled as Anna twisted twigs into Cyrus's hair.

"Shush, everyone," called Zak. "Enough giggling. Trees don't giggle. Any sign of the soldiers?"

"All clear," whispered Cyrus.

Zak turned and waved. "All clear, Ben."

Ben waved back, then turned to face the crowd of Christians who had gathered in Darius's torch-lit courtyard. It was a perfectly calm evening. The moon was full and bright, and the sky was full of stars. "Isn't it a beautiful night?" Ben said to Helena. "Oh, it gladdens my heart to see everyone here."

"Mine too," replied Helena as she squeezed Ben's arm. "Go on, tell them tonight's story."

"Friends!" began Ben.

A hush descended over the courtyard.

"Many of you ask how long we must go on telling the stories of Jesus in secret. Well, one thing is certain, they won't be able to keep us quiet forever."

"Hear, hear!" called Mordecai, and Ben smiled at the old Zealot.

"No more than they could keep a blind beggar quiet the day Jesus passed by.

"Jesus was in the city of Jericho, passing through on his way to Jerusalem. The city was a bustle of people. Children played in the streets. Merchants peddled their wares. The townspeople mingled, laughing and talking, going about their business. Oxen and mules ferried cargo from one part of the city to another. It was a busy old town. And soon a crowd was following Jesus.

"As they left the city gates, Jesus and his disciples came upon a blind man, called Bartimaeus, sitting by the side of the road, begging. As Jesus approached, the blind man heard the commotion and excited voices saying, 'It's Jesus from Nazareth! It's Jesus.'

"Bartimaeus raised his head. The crowd following Jesus got noisier and louder as they approached, and Bartimaeus reached out his bony arms. 'Son of David!' he called. 'Jesus! Help me!'

"The crowd grew noisier still, and Bartimaeus rose to his feet and shouted louder: 'Help me, Son of David!'

"The crowd became angry. 'Hush! Sit down! Be quiet!' they shouted. Several men and women even pulled Bartimaeus back, and he stumbled to the ground.

But Bartimaeus continued to shout, 'Son of David! Help me! Help me!' He stood up again, and a man put his hand over Bartimaeus's mouth. The blind man pushed the hand away and shoved the man. The crowd was getting very angry, very rude.

"Then Jesus stopped in the road and said, 'Call that man over here.'

"Well, the manners of the crowd soon changed, as eager hands tried to help Bartimaeus to stand before Jesus.

"'Cheer up,' said a woman, 'Jesus wants you!'

"A nervous Bartimaeus threw off his dirty old cloak and walked toward Jesus.

"Jesus studied the blind man. 'What do you want me to do for you?'

"Bartimaeus said, simply, "I want to see."

"Jesus stared at him intently. A hush fell over the crowd. Then, finally, Jesus said, 'Go home. Because you have trusted me, you have been made better.'

"Bartimaeus closed his eyes, then opened them again. His eyes were now a clear and bright blue. 'I can see!' he exclaimed. He wiggled his fingers in front of his now teary eyes, and he could see them.

"Bartimaeus turned toward the crowd and smiled at everyone. He could see them. He hugged some, laughing with them as Jesus and the disciples walked on down the road toward Jerusalem."

Mordecai was first on his feet. "Ben, Ben, you are still the best storyteller …"

An urgent knock interrupted his words. Instantly, a hush fell over the crowd. Mordecai pulled a knife from its sheath and stood ready.

Cautiously, Zak opened a secret door, and Darius staggered in.

"Put your knife away," Ben said. "It's Darius."

Darius was out of breath.

"What's wrong?" Ben asked.

"I think I may be too late. There's … going to be a fire … tonight."

"What?" gasped Helena.

"A fire, and a big one. They're moving a catapult into position now. I got here as soon as I could. It's not easy getting out of the Imperial Palace."

"Ben, we're surrounded!" Cyrus yelled from the olive tree.

A troop of torch-bearing soldiers had organized a ring around the Merchant District. The flames lit the night sky, casting ominous shadows.

There was no escape.

## Chapter 7

# Red Sky at Night

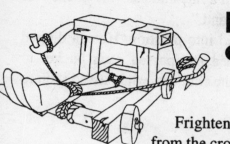

Frightened murmurings escaped from the crowd, and Ben held up his hands. "Friends, please. If we panic it will only make things worse. Stay calm, please."

"I don't think things can get any worse," said Zak anxiously.

He was wrong. Just then, a huge fireball dropped from the sky, landing on a small outbuilding at the back. The building was immediately ablaze.

"Phew! That was a close one," said Zak.

"The next one could be closer," said Mordecai, ever the soldier. "Whoever is in charge of the catapult that sent that fireball was only getting his bearings. He will be making the minor adjustment as we speak."

"Look out!" shouted Zak. "Here comes another!"

A huge ball of fire, blazing a trail of sparks and black smoke, soared through the night sky and exploded on the roof of the house. The Christians were stunned into silence.

37

Zak rallied first, springing into action.

"OK! You all know the drill," he cried. "Ben will get up on the roof. We'll form a line and pass the buckets of water up to him, hand to hand."

The children scrambled into position. Helena dipped water from the well. Then she passed each bucket to Darius, who passed it to the children, who passed it on to other Christians.

"Bucket to you, Anna."

"Over to you, Cyrus."

"That's it, everybody, keep the water coming! Quickly!" Zak yelled. "Well done, Justin, we'll soon have the fire out. How are we doing up there, Ben?"

"Just keep the water coming," Ben called, wiping the sweat from his brow.

Marcus had lined up for the bucket brigade too. But he was too small, and every time he grabbed one of the buckets, it would bump the ground and tip, spilling some of the water.

"Marcus!" yelled Zak. "You're spilling the water! Here, move over, I'll take your place."

Marcus's face fell. "I was doing my best," he said, as he stepped out of the line. Zak ignored him.

Mordecai, carrying some buckets of his own, called out, "I could use your help, Marcus."

Marcus brightened up immediately. He ran to help Zak's uncle fight the raging fire.

# Chapter 8

# Catapult Somersault

On the hill overlooking the Merchant District, Nihilus was rejoicing over the success of his plan.

"Bull's-eye!" he cried as another building burst into flames. "That will teach those Christians to defy Roman law. Reload!"

The soldiers scrambled to load a huge bail of hay into the catapult. Just as they were setting it aflame, Nihilus spotted Tacticus among the soldiers crowding around.

"What are you doing here?" Nihilus growled.

"Hail, Nihilus!" Tacticus said, buttering him up. "How goes the fire?"

"So, Tacticus," sneered Nihilus, "you have decided to come and share in my victory! Well, Nero put me in charge here, and I don't need any help from you. Stay out of my way, and you won't get hurt. I'll show you what it's like to play with fire." Nihilus turned away from Tacticus, laughing at his own joke.

Tacticus stood watching the fires in Rome, wondering what to do next.

His concentration was broken by a munching sound. "Mmm, these apples are good," said Stouticus, pulling another bright red apple from a tree. "Mmm! Delicious!"

*Delicious indeed*, thought Tacticus. *That gives me an idea.*

Tacticus smiled as he strolled toward the horses that were holding the catapult in place. It only took one whiff of the juicy apple on the end of his sword for the horses to react. Like Stouticus, they too knew apples were delicious, and greedily lurched forward, tilting the catapult slightly.

Nihilus was busy looking down upon the fires in the Merchant District. He was pleased with what he saw. "Fire!" he commanded, without looking around. "This time we will burn it all down."

Another fireball shot through the air.

\* \* \*

In a Roman bath on the edge of the Merchant District, a senator was scolding the manager. "Call this a Roman bath? It's freezing!"

"My humblest apologies, my senator," the manager said. "I will turn the fire up right away."

The manager scurried off just as Nihilus's misfired fireball crashed through the window, landing in the senator's bath. The senator disappeared in a cloud of steam.

"Steaming senators!" screamed the senator. "Are you trying to scald me, man?"

But the manager was gone. Spotting the fireball at the last minute, he had already hot-footed it out of the building.

* * *

When the Christians saw where the misfired fireball had landed, they cheered. "I bet you that's Tacticus at work!" Ben cried. With renewed energy, he turned and beat out the last of the flames on Darius's house.

"We did it!" squealed Anna with delight. "The fire's out!"

"Only for the time being." It was a despondent Darius who spoke. "Tacticus won't be able to thwart Nihilus forever."

Ben put his arm around his friend's shoulder. "Darius is right. We'll have to evacuate."

"But how?" grumbled some of the merchants. "We're surrounded!"

"We all knew this day would come," Ben said. "We're prepared. Come on, kids, you know what to do."

"Right, troops," yelled Zak. "Fall in!" Anna, Cyrus, Justin, and Marcus all jumped into action. They knew this was no time for joshing Zak around.

"First, Anna, Cyrus, and Marcus, I want you to disguise that group of merchants over there. Use twigs and leaves. Then show them how to move out as 'bushes.'"

"Yes, Zak," they replied, and quickly got to work.

"Justin and Darius, help those other two into barrels. We'll float them downstream, on the underground river that fills the well."

Ben and Mordecai were already putting Operation Seesaw into action. They quickly moved into position, close to a wall, a plank that had been roped over a barrel. Then Ben and a very fat merchant jumped on the plank, sending Christians, one by one, somersaulting over the Merchant District wall to land safely on a soft mound of hay.

*  *  *

Up on the hill overlooking the Merchant District, Nihilus was barking out orders. "Get rid of those horses. Stake the catapult to the ground this time. That'll keep it secure."

As the soldiers staked the catapult down, Tacticus slinked by and sliced partway through one of the ropes.

"Good, it's ready now. Stand back, everybody. Prepare to fire!" Nihilus cranked back the arm of the catapult. He was about to light the tinder in the bucket when he heard a soft creaking sound that got louder and louder. Just as he bent down to investigate, the rope Tacticus had weakened snapped, causing the catapult to flip over onto its back.

"Get that catapult up NOW!" screamed Nihilus.

His face was scarlet with fury.

# Chapter 9

# Master Horseman

In Darius's courtyard, Mordecai and Helena were disguising a covered wagon. "There," said Helena. "That really looks like a Roman supply carrier, don't you think?"

"It's perfect," said Zak.

"Steady, Hannah," Justin said as he hitched the herbalist's jittery old horse to the disguised wagon. "Steady, old girl. It's going to be all right." He scratched her ear and patted her flank.

Ben pulled his bakery wagon alongside. "How's the evacuation going?"

"Mission accomplished," said Zak proudly. "We're the only ones left."

"Good work, Zak," Ben said. "Now, you and Helena take Mordecai and the kids to the exit point. Justin and I will dress this wagon and meet you back at the bakery."

Helena and the children climbed into the covered wagon while Zak and Mordecai donned Roman uniforms. Then they too climbed aboard, Zak taking the reins and his uncle riding shotgun.

"Hey, Zak!" called Justin. "Go easy on Hannah. Fire makes her very nervous."

"Don't worry." Zak tossed his head and glanced at his uncle. "My father was a master horseman."

"He drove chariots, Zak," Mordecai said, a warning in his voice. "This is a wagon full of children."

"Don't worry, Uncle Mordecai, I know what I'm doing." With that, he slapped the reins against Hannah's back and urged her forward.

\* \* \*

Nihilus impatiently watched his troops tying the catapult to the ground, pounding in stake after stake to hold it securely. "Stouticus, get your back into it. You over there, what are you doing? You're supposed to be pulling that rope, not twiddling with it. Why am I surrounded by such dolts?"

"That's it now, sir," called Stouticus. "The catapult is all set."

"At last, you stupid oaf! If there are any more mistakes, the next flaming projectile to be launched will be *you*."

"That'll teach me to pander to a brute like him," muttered Stouticus under his breath. "I only said that to get a break. Some food, maybe. All I've had to eat in the last hour was a measly apple … or two." Stouticus, his head down, watched as Nihilus ordered the soldiers to begin priming the giant catapult again.

* * *

While the next missile was being loaded, Zak was steering the wagon through the streets of the city. They were approaching the edge of the Merchant District when Anna peeped out at a burning building.

"Helena, how can Nero be so cruel? Doesn't he care about the people of Rome?"

"It's his way of punishing us because we don't always do what he tells us to do."

"Why don't we?" chipped in Marcus.

"Well, sometimes you've got to do what you know is right, even if it gets you into trouble."

Helena settled back a little. Then she launched into a story to keep the children's minds off the danger they were in.

"One time, when Jesus was in the synagogue, he came across a man with a paralyzed hand. It was the Sabbath, the day the Jews are supposed to do no work. A group of Pharisees and members of King Herod's court watched Jesus approach the man. They were watching to see if Jesus was going to break the Sabbath by healing the man.

"When Jesus reached the man, he said, 'Stand up for everybody to see you.'

"The man was pushed toward Jesus, who turned to the worshipers in the synagogue and said, 'What is the right thing to do on the Holy Day? Good or evil? To make someone better, or let him die?'

"No one answered. Jesus was angry because the religious leaders were being so strict and obstinate. They all looked away from Jesus, silent and embarrassed. Jesus then turned to the man and asked him to stretch out his withered hand. The man did so. Slowly, his gnarled fingers began to open, and he could wiggle them. The man smiled with joy when he realized his hand was normal.

"Although the Pharisees admired Jesus' healing powers, many were furious that Jesus had broken their law.

"You see," said Helena, "Jesus knew this would get him into trouble. The Pharisees were so angry they joined with friends of King Herod to plot against Jesus, much in the same way that Nero plots against the Christians of Rome."

# Chapter 10

# Runaway Horse!

Tacticus looked on, helpless.

The catapult was now securely fastened to the ground by dozens of staked ropes, and it was surrounded by guards. There was nothing else Tacticus could do.

Nihilus raised his burning taper and lit another fireball. Then he gave the command: "FIRE!"

The fireball whizzed through the air, exploding in a burst of sparks as it hit another roof.

"Bull's-eye!" shouted Nihilus, gleefully. "Reload!"

"Look at the devastation," said Tacticus to Stouticus. "Soon the whole Merchant District will be on fire."

Stouticus sighed. "It's a pity. They sell some great food down there."

Tacticus just frowned at the soldier. "That's it, Stouticus. That's the Roman way. You only think about yourself."

"Thank you, Tacticus," Stouticus said. He smiled, thinking he'd just received a compliment.

The sky rained a torrent of bright orange fireballs as Nihilus got his giant catapult in full swing.

"Burn, Christians!" he cried. "I, Nihilus, will teach you to worship a carpenter. You will be needing your carpenter to rebuild your houses by the time I've finished with you!"

\* \* \*

Down in the Merchant District, Zak was fighting to keep Hannah moving forward. The smoke and the flames were spooking her. Whinnying and rolling her eyes, she slowed down, then stopped. She tried to back away from a burning building.

"Come on, faster, you old nag!" Zak cried, becoming more and more frustrated.

"Zak!" Mordecai warned. "Justin said you were to go easy on her."

"Yeah, but I can have us out of here in no time," Zak bragged. "Come on! Gee up, Hannah!" He reached for the whip and cracked it over Hannah's head.

"Zak!"

Mordecai's warning came too late. Hannah panicked, rearing up and yanking the reins from Zak's hands. Wheeling around, she charged back the way they had come ... back into the heart of the burning Merchant District.

"The reins! I've lost the reins!" Zak cried.

Anna and Cyrus poked their heads through the front

opening of the wagon. "Shouldn't we be going the other way?" Cyrus asked.

"Tell that to Hannah. Whooooaa!" Zak cried, hanging on to the seat with both hands as the wagon rocketed down the street, out of control.

* * *

In Darius's courtyard, Ben and Justin were finishing the disguise for their wagon. "That's it," Ben said. "Just in time, too. The fireballs are coming in thick and fast."

Justin, looking down the street, spotted Hannah galloping their way.

"Ben!" Justin cried.

Ben turned in time to see Hannah gallop past with the wagon rocking dangerously behind her. "What in the world?"

"They're heading right into the fire!" Justin shouted.

"Ben! Help us!" Helena and the children cried.

Quickly, Ben and Justin climbed aboard the bakery wagon and Ben snapped the reins over the horse's back. The horse lunged forward, as if sensing the urgency.

They had to stop Hannah.

She was headed right for the center of the blaze.

## Chapter 11

# Lyre, Lyre, Pantheon Fire

In his Imperial Palace, Nero was stroking his lyre and composing songs as he watched the orange glow from the distant fire spread and light up the night sky.

> *"Fire burn bright,*
> *fire burn strong.*
> *Soon I will build*
> *my new pantheon."*

"Marvelous," Nero crowed. "This is marvelous. Oh, I do love a good fire. Look, Snivilus. Look how the sparks soar high into the sky. And see, there goes another fireball. It is like a giant shooting star leaving a blazing trail in its wake. Oh, that Nihilus is so clever, almost more clever than I."

"No, Nero, never," Snivilus lied. "No one is cleverer than the cleverest Nero there ever was."

"We must remember to reward Nihilus. The Legion of Honor or something. Anything will do. These centurions are easily pleased."

"Of course, Nero. Any commendation from you is an honor."

"Really, Snivilus? Is that really the case?"

"Of course, oh Excellent One."

"Then I ordain you Snivilus Grovelus …"

Snivilus preened himself expectantly. "Yes?"

"Snivilus Grovelus, GLT."

"GLT? Ah, why thank you, Caesar. Thank you, Your Greatness."

"You're welcome." Nero smiled.

Snivilus hesitated. Then quickly he asked, "May I inquire what GLT stands for, your Excellent Cleverness, oh Great Emperor of the Civilized World?"

Nero smiled even more broadly, snickered, then laughed out loud. "It stands for 'Groveling Little Toad.'"

"Oh!"

"Well, Snivilus? Aren't you going to thank me?"

"Of course, Great One. Thank you."

"Hmm, Snivilus," Nero said, rubbing his chin thoughtfully. "You don't seem too grateful. I wonder, do you think the lions are hungry?"

Snivilus snapped to attention. "I don't know, oh Wonderful One, oh Splendid Singer of the World's Best-Written Songs, oh High Emperor of the Imperial Roman Empire, oh Magnificent, oh …"

As the hungry lions roared in the distance, Snivilus continued to earn his new commendation long into the night.

# Chapter 12

# Wheels on Fire

Zak's wagon, pulled by a runaway horse, rocketed down the street directly into the heart of the Merchant District. All around was chaos. People were fleeing from their burning homes and shops, carrying whatever they could. Buildings were burning on all sides. Smoke filled the air and stung their lungs.

"I have to get the reins," Zak shouted to his Uncle Mordecai. He leaned out of the wagon, dangerously close to Hannah's pounding hooves.

"I ... can't ... quite ... reach ... the reins," Zak groaned.

"Here," Mordecai said. "Take my hand!"

Clutching Mordecai's hand, Zak managed to lean out farther and grab the reins. "Got them!" he cried triumphantly.

Zak swung back into the driver's seat. "Thanks, Uncle Mordecai. Now, horse, I'll show you who's boss."

"Take it easy, Zak. You know what happened the last time."

"Hannah!" yelled Zak as he pulled on the reins. "Stop right now!"

But he pulled too hard, and the reins snapped in two where they had been dragged on the ground. Zak shot an embarrassed look at his uncle.

"Zak," sighed Mordecai, "I did tell you to be careful."

"M-M-Mordecai! Zak!" called Helena from the back of the wagon. "W-w-w-what's g-g-g-going on? The chi-chi-children and I are being sh-sh-shaken around in the back here."

"Sorry, Helena, but we have a problem."

Helena, Anna, Cyrus, and Marcus bounced about in the wagon as they looked out the black. "Look!" shouted Cyrus. "It's B-B-Ben and Justin."

"Hold on, kids," called Ben.

"W-we're t-t-trying!"

"Zak!" shouted Justin as they pulled alongside. "Hang on! I'll try to calm Hannah down."

Whipping his horse, Ben inched his wagon alongside the runaway horse. Justin leaned over.

"Okay, Ben," Justin called, "just a little closer. Let me speak to her. That's it. Whoa, girl! Whoa! Come on, Hannah, I have an apple. Whoa!"

But Hannah continued to run full speed, rolling her eyes and snorting, tossing her head in a frenzy.

Justin pulled back into the wagon. "She's not listening. She's terrified. I *told* Zak to be careful."

"Never mind that," said Ben, "we must help them." As

the two wagons rolled on side by side, Ben yelled, "Helena, Anna, pull the canopy off the wagon!"

"Why?"

"You'll have to jump!"

Mordecai helped Helena and Anna roll back the cover on the wagon.

"Children first," said Helena. "Anna and Cyrus, you hold Marcus's hand."

"Okay," said Cyrus. "Everybody ready?"

Marcus gulped as he watched the gap between the two wagons opening and closing. "I'm ready," he said bravely.

"Okay, on a count of three."

"One, two, … six!" yelled Marcus, and Anna and Cyrus leaped into Ben's wagon, hauling Marcus with them.

"All right, Helena," called Justin. "You're next."

"Can't you get closer, Ben?" said Helena, looking at the gap.

"Helena, the wagons are almost touching," Ben reassured her. "If I get any closer, I'll be driving *your* wagon."

"Oh, dear," said Helena. "I've never done anything like this before."

"Just don't look down!" Marcus shouted.

Flanked by Mordecai and Zak, Helena steadied herself, getting ready to jump.

Suddenly, a fireball exploded right in front of the

horses. Hannah reared up in fright, then jumped over the flaming hay, breaking her harness loose from the wagon. At that same moment, Helena and Mordecai jumped, tumbling into Ben's wagon.

Zak was left behind.

His now-horseless wagon rolled right into the fireball, tipped up on two wheels, and burst into flames.

"Help!" Zak screamed, as the wagon dropped back onto all four wheels.

Out of control and on fire, Zak's wagon barreled down a hill straight toward a massive wall of flames ... a burning building at the bottom.

Ben struggled to maneuver his wagon back alongside the horseless wagon. "Hold on, Zak, I'm coming. When I yell, you better jump. Now, Zak!"

Zak leaped aboard Ben's wagon as Ben jerked the reins sharply and veered wildly into an alleyway. The horseless wagon smashed into the burning building, and was lost in a mass of flames and smoke and rubble as the building collapsed.

"Wow!" said a relieved Zak. "That was too close!"

"Hey, Ben," said Mordecai, "did they teach you to drive like that in baker's school?"

"Yes, but the ovens were much smaller."

"I know what you mean," replied Mordecai. "Let's get out of this cauldron. The heat is coming our way."

"Then hold tight, everyone. The ride isn't over yet. Hey, Justin. Look, there's Hannah escaping."

# Chapter 13

# Fire Down Below

On a hill high above the city, Nihilus and Tacticus stood watching as the catapult flung yet another fireball into the already inferno-like Merchant District.

"Ha!" laughed Nihilus. "I like fires almost as much as Nero. Look at those fools trying to save their houses. They look just like ants from up here, don't you think?"

"They look more like people to me," Tacticus said quietly.

"Huh!" Nihilus grunted, flashing a distrustful look at his colleague. Then he called out to his men, "Keep firing! Reload, and no slacking!"

\* \* \*

In the city below, Ben was struggling to steer his overloaded wagon through the chaotic streets. Coughing and choking from the smoke, the children held their sleeves to their faces.

Justin, up on the bench beside Ben, peered through the flames and smoke. "There has to be some way out of here," he cried.

The wagon slid to a stop at the center of an intersection near a tall statue of a Roman archer. With growing fear, Ben and Justin looked around. The exits were all closed by flames. Every building they could see was on fire. Ben turned the wagon around, hoping to go back the way he'd come, when suddenly a burning building collapsed onto the street, blocking their escape.

"We're trapped!" Justin cried.

"Look out!" shouted Helena, as another building collapsed at the other end of the intersection. A jumble of flaming rubble scattered all around them.

"Quickly!" shouted Ben. "Come with me!"

Ben dipped his helmet into a pool of water at the statue's base and flung the water at the burning debris. Zak and Mordecai did the same. Helena and the children used clay pots from the wagon.

"Ben, the smoke is bad," Anna said, coughing and wiping away tears with sooty hands. "Look! That building there!"

"Just keep the water coming, Anna."

Zak, who was working with Mordecai, turned to him and said, "Uncle Mordecai, I'm so sorry. This is all my fault."

"Chin up, Zak, I've been in tighter scrapes than this." He looked up just as another fireball flew overhead. "Duck!" he cried. He and Zak covered their heads and dove behind the wagon.

"Tighter, yes, but I bet none quite so warm," Zak said,

picking himself up. "I just wanted to impress you, that's all," he said sheepishly.

"Impress me? So that's why you've been acting so strangely."

"I ... I don't deserve to wear my father's medallion. Here, take it back." Zak began to remove the medallion from his neck.

"Nonsense, Zak!" Mordecai said, laying a hand on his arm. "Your father was a great leader. That is true. But he wasn't *born* a great leader. He became one over time ... and you will too."

"I ... I will?"

"Of course. Once you have learned to think a little before leaping into action."

"Look out!" yelled Cyrus. "Here comes another fireball!"

"And another!" yelled Justin. "They're shooting at *us*!"

A fireball toppled another building, scattering more flames and rubble near the statue. Pulling the horse and wagon behind him, Ben shouted, "Quickly, everyone, get over to the statue and stand in the water! It's our only chance!"

Everyone followed Ben into the fountain. "All right, are we all here? Mordecai, Helena, Zak, Justin, and Marcus. Where's Cyrus?"

"He was fighting the fire over there. He must be trapped! I can't see him! There's so much smoke!" Anna cried.

Just then they heard Cyrus's voice. "Ben!" *Cough, cough.* "Ben! Where are you?"

"Cyrus! Over here!" Ben cried. "At the base of the fountain. By the archer."

As Cyrus ran through the black smoke, some timbers crashed down in front of him. But Cyrus was too nimble to be caught. His circus training came in handy, and he skipped and wove his way out of the flames.

"That's it, good boy!" shouted Ben encouragingly. He grabbed the grubby Cyrus by the hand and pulled him into the water with the rest of them.

Next to the statue, flames crackled and popped as they licked their way up a tall building. Justin cried, "If that building goes, we're all done for!"

Zak looked up to the sky. "Oh, Father," he said, "if only you were here now. You would know what to do. I've let everyone down."

Tears stung his eyes. Then, for the first time, he noticed the statue. The stone archer was pointing up to an unknown foe. Imagining the arrow's path, Zak saw a possible destination.

Suddenly, he had an idea. "Cyrus, do you think you could climb to the top of that statue?"

"Sure. Why?"

"I've got an idea. Justin, fetch me the rope from the cart. It's a long shot, but it might work. Anna, I'll need your help too."

# Chapter 14

# Double Trouble

Above the city, Tacticus and Stouticus stood watching as the city burned.

"Phew!" Stouticus sighed, wiping his brow. "This old catapult is getting red hot. You could roast a goose on the swing arm."

Tacticus nodded impatiently. "Yes, Stouticus, so you could. So you could."

"I don't suppose you have one, do you? Roast goose sounds so good. I am getting a bit peckish. All this catapulting is no picnic."

Tacticus just smiled at the portly soldier. Stouticus's comment about the heat of the swing arm had given him an idea.

"Hey, Nihilus, why don't you speed things up a bit by doubling the load?" Tacticus shouted.

"I'm in charge of this operation, Tacticus. I'll give the orders!"

Nihilus turned back to the catapult and shouted to Stouticus, "Double the load!"

\* \* \*

In the center of the Merchant District, Zak was giving instructions to Cyrus, who had shimmied up the statue. "That's it, Cyrus. Good! Now tie the rope onto the bow."

"Be careful, Cyrus," Helena cried anxiously.

Zak went on giving orders. "Now you, Anna, tie the other end of the rope to the bottom of the bow. ... That's it. Well done."

"Phew!" said Ben, mopping his brow. "I don't know if this plan of Zak's is going to work, but I sure hope so. It's getting hot here ... and look, that last building is on the verge of collapse. Quickly, Zak, we're running out of time!"

* * *

Back on the hill, Nihilus was gloating. "That was a great idea of mine," he said to no one in particular. "With this extra load we will soon have the area cleared. Prepare to fire!"

"Sir," interrupted Stouticus, "I don't think we ..."

"You're not here to think. You're here to act. Now fire the catapult."

"But, sir ... I smell something burning," said Stouticus, his face creased with worry.

"Of course you do, that's because it is. I said *fire*!"

"No, I mean ..." Nihilus shoved Stouticus out of the way and released the firing trigger. The arm of the catapult swung forward, snapping where it had burned, and dropping its burning fireball back onto itself.

Nihilus shrieked as his favorite weapon burst into flames. "Fire! My beautiful catapult is on fire!"

"I tried to tell you, sir, but …"

"Shut up, Stouticus, and give me that bucket!"

"But sir, that's …"

Before Stouticus could finish his sentence, Nihilus threw the contents of the bucket over the catapult. There was an almighty whooshing sound, followed by a crackling roar, as the entire catapult went up in flames.

"… oil," Stouticus said softly, finishing his warning.

"My catapult!" Nihilus watched in anger as his great weapon went up in flames. Through the smoke, he caught a glimpse of Tacticus. The other soldier gave him the slightest of smiles, then turned and walked away.

\* \* \*

Ben could see the blaze on top of the hill. He turned to Mordecai. "I wonder what that is."

"I don't know," said Mordecai.

"Okay, everyone," Zak called. "I've looped the rope around this bust of Nero. Help me to lift it up."

Zak, Mordecai, Ben, Helena, and even little Marcus struggled to move the bust of Nero. "We're going to use the bust as an arrow," Zak explained. "Just a little to the left … now a little lower … hold it! Now everyone, the bowstring. We have to pull it back."

They all drew back the improvised bowstring. The metal prongs of the statue's bow bent slightly as the gang pulled on the rope.

"Tighter!" called Zak. "Tighter!"

They were almost backing into the fire. The heat was intense. Zak wiped the smoke and sweat from his eyes, then followed the line of the bust, carefully taking aim.

"I *think* the bust is directed at the aqueduct," said Zak to Mordecai. "But what if I miss again?"

"Then I was proud just to know you!" Mordecai said. "Give it your best shot. That's all anyone can do."

Zak took a deep breath. The flaming building above them began to totter, dropping chunks of fiery wood all around them.

"Now!" yelled Zak.

Everyone released the bust. It rocketed up, heading straight for the aqueduct, and smashed into the side. Stones flew in all directions.

"Bull's-eye!" shouted Cyrus. "Stand by for the deluge!"

Everyone cheered as water poured out of the hole in the side of the aqueduct and cascaded down upon them.

"You did it, Zak, you did it!" cried Anna, Cyrus, and Justin in unison.

Zak just grinned.

Helena and Marcus held hands and splashed joyfully in the pool, now overflowing with water. The others hooted and danced as the water extinguished the fires on the ground around them.

"I'm wet!" roared Ben, as he stood directly under the

aqueduct's waterfall. "Gloriously, joyfully, hopelessly wet!"

Mordecai turned to his nephew. "Zak, now that's a shot even your father would have been proud of. Come here."

Everyone cheered as Mordecai wrapped his arms around his nephew and ruffled a hand through his hair.